AMAL'S EID

WORDS BY: AMY MARANVILLE   ILLUSTRATED BY: JOSHUA STEVENS

www.mascotbooks.com | www.bharatbabies.com

Amal's Eid

For more information, please contact:
Mascot Books | 560 Herndon Parkway #120 | Herndon, VA 20170
info@mascotbooks.com

Library of Congress Control Number: 2015907724

CPSIA Code: PRT0615A
ISBN-13: 978-1-63177-298-6

Printed in the United States

To all my friends and family.

- Josh

For Will, for his endless support and love.

- Amy

For Amma. Thanks for always telling me a story.

- Sailaja

My name is Amal and Eid is my favorite holiday.

Eid is always at the end of the month of Ramadan. For all of Ramadan, we fast during the day.

But on Eid, we eat lots and lots of food! My mother and aunt are in the kitchen all week making the food for our feast. Youssef and I like to watch them make the sweets because Auntie always sneaks us extra *cham cham* behind our mother's back.

For Eid, we get new clothes. My brother and I get to choose our *salwaar kameez*, a special tunic and long pants. Plus hats to match!

We give gifts. This year, I wrote a poem for my father and drew a picture for my mother. I gave my brother Youssef a rock for his collection.

We listen to music.

Sometimes, we sing along.

But my favorite part of Eid is when my grandparents come to see us. They live far away, so they can't come until dinnertime. Before they arrive, we make the house extra tidy and dress in our special clothes.

When my *Nana* and *Nani* arrive, the house gets loud and crowded and everyone shouts over each other to be heard. Then we sit down to eat around our big table.

At night, before we go to bed, my grandmother and grandfather take turns telling us stories. It's hard to stay awake after such a long day, but the stories are too wonderful to sleep through.

First, my grandmother tells us about Ramadan. "Ramadan," she says, "is a time for us to reflect on the year. While the sun is shining, we do not eat or drink. We pray and try to be better people."

She tells us about the first Ramadan she remembers from her childhood. "I was so hungry!" she laughs. "But I also felt important and honored to be a grownup, fasting with all my relatives."

Usually, children don't fast for Ramadan. But my parents promised I could try next year, when I am 12. I think about that, while I doze in my mother's lap.

Then our grandfather teases my grandmother about her *Iftar*, the meal eaten at the end of the day during Ramadan. "She made the best sweets in the village," he says.

This makes all of us hungry again, so my mother passes out bowls of my grandmother's famous gulab jamun on trays. I dip my spoon in the bowl and break apart the milky balls coated in sweet syrup.

While we eat,
we talk about
what we learned during
Ramadan and what we hope to
do better next year. My brother says
he wants to get better at math. I say
I want to improve my spelling and
work on my temper.

We all help clean up the dishes.

Then we settle down and sing and play, happy to be together.

After a while,

We kiss and hug goodnight, and go to bed with full bellies and happy hearts.

And we dream of next year.

THE END

About the Author

Amy Maranville has a Bachelor of Arts in English literature and anthropology from Smith College, and a Master's in Children's Literature from Simmons College in Boston. She is a passionate believer in the importance of diversity in the books we give to our children and is proud to present positive images of diversity in her stories. Amy lives in Somerville, Massachusetts with her husband, young son, and beloved basset hound.

About the Illustrator

Joshua Stevens loves using his background in animation to help create strong and interesting characters and fun designs. Variety is the spice of life and he's always looking to try new things to do! To see infrequent updates on what Josh is currently up to and focusing on, check out his art blog at amazingtrout.tumblr.com.